Virginia J. Kent

Lessons for Little Folks 1877

A merry Christmas and happy New Year to you all 1878

Virginia J. Kent

Lessons for Little Folks 1877
A merry Christmas and happy New Year to you all 1878

ISBN/EAN: 9783337381844

Printed in Europe, USA, Canada, Australia, Japan

Cover: Foto ©Andreas Hilbeck / pixelio.de

More available books at **www.hansebooks.com**

1877.

A

Merry Christmas

—AND—

Happy New Year

To You All.

1878.

CHICAGO:
PUBLISHED BY THE AUTHOR.
1877.

R. R. M'CABE & CO.,
PRINTERS,
57 Washington St., Chicago.

THESE lessons and hymns have nearly all been prepared for and used in my little classes from time to time. I now arrange them as a Christmas gift for the little ones at present under my care. Should they reach "others not of this fold," may they be a blessing in some way to each little heart! I send also with the gift, greeting to all who love to feed the lambs of the flock—to parents, to whom is granted the privilege of first impressing the child's heart; and to teachers, who should be "instant in season and out of season," adding line upon line, precept upon precept, here a little and there a little, and never be weary in well doing, knowing that the seed sown *now* will sooner or later ripen into a golden harvest. And now a word to my

DEAR CHILDREN:

Will you accept from your loving teacher this little book, and try to remember *all* the good things contained in its pages, but particularly those from God's own book? Hide them away in your heart, that you may be wise unto salvation.

Your affectionate teacher,

VIRGINIA J. KENT.

Bless
the Lord, O my
soul; and all
that is within
me, bless
His Holy name.
Bless
the Lord, O my
soul, and
forget not all
His benefits.

Psalm ciii. 1, 2.

4

CHRISTMAS HYMN.

WHILE shepherds watched their flocks by night,
　　All seated on the ground,
　The angel of the Lord came down,
　　And glory shone around.

"Fear not," said he, for mighty dread
　Had seized their troubled mind:
"Glad tidings of great joy I bring
　To you and all mankind.

"To you in David's town, this day,
　Is born in David's line,
A Saviour who is Christ the Lord;
　And this shall be the sign:

"The heavenly Babe you there shall find
　To human view displayed,
All meanly wrapt in swathing bands,
　And in a manger laid."

Thus spoke the seraph, and forthwith
　Appeared a shining throng
Of angels praising God, who thus
　Addressed their joyful song:

"All glory be to God on high,
　And to the earth be peace,
Good will henceforth from heaven to men
　Begin and never cease."

Glory
to God in the highest, and on earth peace, good will to men.

Luke ii. 14.

6

THE OLD YEAR.

HE steals away so quietly,
   I cannot bid him stay,
To ask the record of the past
He marked from day to day.

Yet every day and every hour
   Has in its buried past,
Something of good or evil done,
   Which must forever last.

Dear Father, take the record, *all*
   Of 1877;
Forgive the evil, let the good
   Be treasured up in heaven.

Watch, therefore, for ye know not the day nor the hour when the Son of man cometh.

THE NEW YEAR.

WELCOME! we greet thee, for we know
 A Father's generous hand
Has sent thee, full of hope and cheer,
 To this our favored land.

The cloud, the sunshine, and the rain,
 The seed and harvest days,
Shall all be ours, as 'twas of old.
 To Him we give the praise.

Help us to honor Thee, O Lord—
 Thy goodness is so great—
And faithful, loving children be,
 In 1878.

A PROMISE.

If ye be willing and obedient, ye shall eat the good of the land.

Isa. i. 19.

A MORNING PRAYER.

JESUS, with the light of day,
We, Thy little ones, would pray:

From all evil keep us free,

Save us from displeasing Thee;

Every day and every hour,

Save us by Thy mighty power:

And when all our days are o'er,

We will praise Thee, evermore!

When thou prayest, enter into thy closet, and when thou hast shut thy door, pray to thy Father which is in secret.

Matt. vi. 6.

12

AN EVENING PRAYER.

——— —

DEAR Father, at the evening hour,
  As at the morning light,
Thy little one comes asking Thee
  To keep her (him) through the night.

Forgive all naughty words or deeds
  I've said or done to-day,
And make me, Lord, a better child;
  Most humbly do I pray.

Bless mamma, papa, all my friends,
  And may we all love Thee.
I ask it all for Jesus' sake;
  To Him the praise shall be.

Evening, and
morning, and at
noon,
will I pray, and
cry aloud;
and He shall
hear my voice.

Psalm lv. 17.

LITTLE THINGS.

TWO little eyes, to look to God;

Two little ears, to hear His Word;

Two little feet, to walk in His ways;

Two hands, to work for Him all my days;

One little tongue, to speak His truth;

One little heart for Him, now in my youth.

Take them, dear Jesus, and let them be

Always obedient and true to Thee.

Even so it is not the will of your Father which is in Heaven, that one of these little ones should perish.

A PRAYER AT THE OPENING

OF SUNDAY SCHOOL.

DEAR Father, we, Thy little ones,

Assemble here to-day,

To hear of Jesus' love to us,

And learn to praise and pray.

O help *me* and my schoolmates dear

Remember that the Lord is here.

Enter into
His gates with
thanksgiving,
and
into His courts
with praise;
Be thankful
unto Him,
and bless His
name.

Psalm c. 4

A PRAYER AT THE CLOSING

OF SUNDAY SCHOOL.

DEAR Father, now, before we part,

  Receive our humble prayer,

And fill with love each little heart;

  Go with us everywhere.

O, may we ever watchful be!

Keep us, O, keep us near to Thee!

I will instruct thee, and teach thee in the way which thou shalt go; I will guide thee with Mine eye.

Psalm. xxxii. 8.

A SUNDAY SCHOOL EXERCISE

I CLOSE my eyes and look within,
And lo! my heart is full of sin!
I *raise* my eyes and look above,
And Jesus, with His heart of love,
Looks down in pity on His child;
Although I'm wayward, wandering, wild,
He calls me back, and freely gives
Me pardon, and my heart receives.

Like as
a father pitieth
his children,
so the Lord piti-
eth them
that fear Him.

Psalm ciii. 13.

Who for-
giveth all thine
iniquities.

Psalm ciii. 3.

SOMETHING TO THINK ABOUT.

IF you love Me, Jesus said,
    You must show it.
If you really love the Saviour,
    You will know it.
If you love your little brother,
Your father, or your mother,
You don't have to ask *another*
      If it's so ;
      For you know
That your hearts are bound together,
      And your love
      You can prove,
By cheerfully obeying each request.
Then prove your love for Jesus,
      As He said,
By keeping His commandments,
      And be led
By His gentle, loving spirit ;
And trusting in His merit,
You at last will enter into His rest.

If ye love Me, keep My com-mandments.

John xiv. 15.

Serve the Lord with gladness.

Psalm c. 2.

SOMETHING TO REMEMBER.

WHENEVER the church is opened for
    prayer,
Satan is about the first to be there;
He watches the coming of all, and soon sees
Whom he can trouble and whom he can please.

But Jesus has told us that, even where two
Or three go to worship, He always goes, too;
He will teach them to pray and grant their
    request,
And give to His children just what is best.

Let us cling to Him closely, and Satan will fly,
For he never can harm us when Jesus is nigh;
Let us look unto Him and be saved from all
    sin,
And be ready to go when He says "Enter in."

25

God
is a Spirit, and they that worship Him must worship Him in spirit and in truth.

John iv. 24.

DAYS OF THE WEEK.

EVEN bright jewels our Father above
    Hath given His children, in mercy and
        love:
    Beautiful jewels set in gold
For the rich and poor, the young and the old.
But *one* He asks may to Him be given,
That each may have some treasure in Heaven.

These jewels are days, and we are blest
With hours for labor and hours for rest.
Let us work with all zeal, be fervent in spirit,
That we may the kingdom of Heaven inherit.

S–aviour of sinners, O, hear while we pray!
M–aster, O lead us and guide us alway!
T–he Lord is my Shepherd, and He will
        provide;
W–atchful and prayerful, I'll keep by His side.
T–here is room for no idler in the vineyard to
        wait—
F–aithful workers are needed, the harvest is
        great—
S–uch only shall enter the beautiful gate.

Fear not, little flock, for it is your Father's good pleasure to give you the kingdom.

Luke xii. 32.

THE SEVEN DAYS OF THE WEEK.

MONDAY, remember that God is your
Friend;

TUESDAY, with care your hours to spend;

WEDNESDAY, remember that "God is
love;"

THURSDAY, your love for Him to prove;

FRIDAY, remember the narrow way;

SATURDAY, time is passing away;

SUNDAY, remember from labor to rest—

'Tis God's holy day, the sweetest and best.

29

Not sloth-ful in business; fervent in spirit; serv-ing the Lord.

Rom. xii. 11.

Remember the Sabbath day to keep it holy.

Ex. xx. 8.

A PROMISE.

JESUS has said it,

Therefore it is true—

The Holy Spirit

Abideth with you.

Jesus has said it;

O, do not grieve

The Holy Spirit,

Nor tempt Him to leave.

I will pray
the Father, and
He
shall give you
another
Comforter, that
He may
abide with you
forever.

John xiv. 16.

DIALOGUE IN VERSE.

SUCH a little one as I,
Will not Jesus pass me by?

    No; for in His word we read,
    He His little ones will lead.

I am often naughty, too;
Then I know not what to do.

    Jesus tells us, if we pray,
    He will take our sins away.

But His throne is up so high,
Far above the starry sky.

    Yet He's never far away
    From His children when they pray.

Together—

    Let us, then, His word believe,
    Nor His gentle Spirit grieve.
    Jesus, Master, from above,
    Fill our little hearts with love.

Jesus said, Suffer the little children to come unto Me, and forbid them not, for of such is the kingdom of Heaven.

Mark x. 14.

HAPPY LITTLE CHILDREN.

HAPPY little children
   All the time are we;
Every one can truly say,
   " Jesus cares for me."

Happy little children,
   With a spirit free;
In our little hearts we say,
   " Jesus loveth me."

Happy little children
   May we always be,
Saying from our little hearts,
   " Jesus, we love thee."

Happy little children ;
   When we come to die,
We shall have a home above,
   With Jesus, in the sky.

35

I love them that love Me, and those that seek Me early shall find Me.

JESUS HAS A

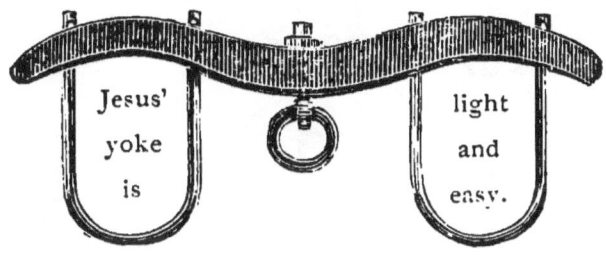

Jesus' yoke is — light and easy.

SATAN HAS A

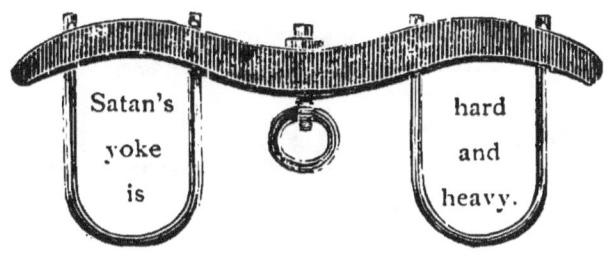

Satan's yoke is — hard and heavy.

Whose shall we wear?

Take my
yoke upon you
and
learn of Me, for
I am
meek and lowly
in heart,
and ye shall find
rest
unto your souls.

Matt. xi. 24.

JESUS SAID:

I will  and

guide lead thee

In the way of all truth.

———

SATAN SAYS:

Follow me, and I will give you all the

riches  the

of world.

———

Whom shall we follow?

Jesus said,

I am the way,

the truth,

and the life.

John xiv. 6.

JESUS SAID:

I am   and

the   know

good   my

Shepherd   sheep;

I lay down my life for my sheep.

SATAN IS THE

who   devours

destroys   the

and   sheep.

The wolf cometh but for to kill.

For
the Son of man
is come to
save that which
was lost.

Matt. xviii. 11.

BEHOLD  of

the God,

That taketh away the sin of the world.

SATAN  like

goeth a

about roaring

Seeking whom he may devour.

He
shall feed His
flock like
a shepherd; He
shall
gather the
lambs
with His arm
and
carry them in
His bosom.

Isa. xl. 11.

JESUS WANTS YOUR

and

Love, Purity,
Joy, Kindness,
Peace, Patience,
Long-Suffering,
H mility,
Zeal.

fill it

will

with

"I want your heart, dear children,
I want your heart to-day."

SATAN WANTS YOUR

He

Pride, Anger,
Malice, Sloth,
Hatred, Deceit,
Covetousness,
Impatience,
Envy.

fill it

will

with

Who shall have it?

45

The heart is deceitful above all things, and desperately wicked; who can know it? I the Lord search the heart.

Jer. xvii. 9, 10.

JESUS SAID:

I am 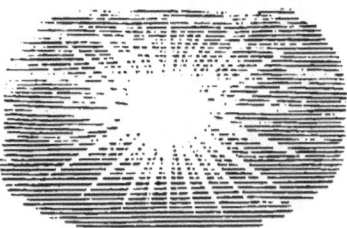 of

the the

light world:

he that followeth Me shall have the
light of life.

John viii. 12.

SATAN LOVES DARKNESS.

His  bear

works the

will not light.

Shall we be in the light with Christ, or
in the dark with Satan?

Every
one that doeth
evil
hateth the
light,
neither cometh
to the light.

John iii. 20.

I OUGHT TO

PRAY often;

Read my Bible daily;

Obey my parents;

Love and obey God;

Love my neighbor;

Repent of sin;

Be converted;

Have a pure heart;

Live a pure life

Blessed

are the pure in

heart,

for they shall

see God.

Matt. v. 8.

OBEDIENCE TO PARENTS.

HONOR thy father and thy mother, that thy days may be long upon the land which the Lord thy God giveth thee.

Fifth Commandment. Ex. xx. 12.

Honor thy father and mother, which is the first commandment with promise.

Eph. vi. 2.

Children, obey your parents in the Lord, for this is right.

Eph. vi. 1.

Children, obey your parents in all things, for this is well pleasing unto the Lord.

Col. iii. 20.

A wise son maketh a glad father; but a foolish son is the heaviness of his mother.

GOD'S CARE.

HOW many are the little stars
    That stud the evening sky,
And shine so brightly all the night,
    Like diamonds, up so high!

How many are the blades of grass
    That spring beneath our feet!
And flowers unnumbered meet our gaze,
    So full of fragrance sweet.

How many little drops of rain
    Fall on the thirsty ground,
And make the fruit and golden grain
    So richly to abound!

And so unnumbered blessings come
  To each of us below—
As many as the stars above,
  And flowers beneath that grow.

The sunshine falls upon our path,
  The hours come and go,
And yet we scarcely have a thought
  From whence these blessings flow.

Dear Father, may we love Thee more,
  Who every need supplies,
And render up ourselves to Thee
  A willing sacrifice!

HOW TO WORSHIP GOD.

WHEN I enter the house of prayer,
　I must remember that God is there;
I must respectful and quiet be,
Because it is written, "God seeth me."

In closing my eyes to offer prayer
To God, who is here and everywhere,
I must solemn and earnest be,
Because it is written, " He listeneth to me."

If I have a wicked thought within,
Or am clinging to any secret sin,
My words will only mockery be,
Because it is written, " He knoweth me."

55

God cares for the flowers, the birds, the
 trees,

And surely we are of more value than
 these ;

Then I will not troubled or anxious be,

Because it is written, " He loveth me."

And then in His holy Word we read

That He will supply our every need ;

And so, I must never distrustful be,

Because it is written, " He careth for me."

Our footsteps, too, He has promised to
 guide,

And ever keep near His children's side ;

O, may I never unfaithful be,

Because it is written, " He leadeth me ! "

56

THE CLOCK.

 HEAR the clock strike, and what does it
    say?
One, Two, Three, Four, Five, Six! A
    beautiful day!
Again it strikes, Seven! and brightly the sun
Is shining, and work for the day has begun.
I hear it at Eight, as clear as a bell;
It says, " I have wonderful things to tell.
Don't waste any moments; they're not yours,
    nor mine;
See how quickly they pass. [I hear it strike
    Nine!]
Not slothful in business! hear this, idle men!

Four hours are lost! [And then it strikes Ten!]
No lazy ones enter the kingdom of heaven;"
And it rings out in warning the number
    Eleven!
Why it's *noon*, I declare, and while we all rest,
I hear the Clock *ticking* and *ticking* its best.
It never gets tired, *its* work's never done;
But it does rest a *little;* hark, it only strikes
    One!
O, I can't keep up with it, whatever I do;
Just while I am talking, again it strikes Two!
Then quickly comes Three, and then it is Four!
The hours seem shorter and shorter, I'm sure.
These moments *are* precious; O, how we
    should strive
To improve each one faithfully! *One, Two,*
    Three, Four, FIVE!
As through the day, so all through the night,
The clock ticks and strikes, till again it is light;
And then at the dawn begins over again
To ring out the hours, for pleasure and pain.

A PRAYER.

HEAVENLY Father, bend thine ear,
  And thy little children hear;
  Take away our every sin,
  Cleanse our hearts, and enter in!

Stay with us, and let us be
Glad to love and follow Thee;
Teach us how to watch and pray,
Lead us in the narrow way.

May we never weary be
Till the golden gate we see;
Father, then thy children take
Home to heaven, for Jesus' sake!

Thou
shalt guide me
with thy
counsel, and
afterward
receive me to
glory.

Psalm lxxiii. 24.

LESSONS ON THE COMMAND-MENTS.

HOW many Commandments are there?
Ten.
Who gave them to us?
God.
How were they sent?
Through Moses.
On what were they written?
Two tables of stone.
How were they written?
By the finger of God?
What is the First Commandment?
Thou shalt have no other gods before Me.
What does it mean, to have " no other god?"
Not to love anything *more* than God; to please Him first in all things; to love Him better than all our friends, or all earthly good— yes, even better than our own lives.
Why should we do this?
Because He has made us, and has given us

61

everything we possess, and only asks us to love Him best in return for all He has done.

[The teacher or parent can here speak of different kinds of gods—idols of the heathen, home idols, friends, money, self, etc.—stating how and why they draw our hearts from God.]

Sing to the tune "St. Louis"—

> Jesus, help me from this day,
> Thy commandments to obey;
> May I give Thee all my heart,
> And with every evil part.

What is the Second Commandment?

Thou shalt not make to thyself any graven image, nor the likeness of anything that is in heaven above, or in the earth beneath, or in the water under the earth. Thou shalt not bow down thyself to them, nor serve them; for I the Lord thy God am a jealous God, visiting the iniquity of the fathers upon the children unto the third and fourth generation of them that hate Me, and showing mercy unto thousands of them that love Me and keep My commandments.

[Explain how, even in our day, many worship and pray to images and pictures.]

Why does this displease God?

Because He is a jealous God, and wants us to love and worship Him alone.

Has He a right to our worship?

He has; for He made us, and when we sinned He sent His only Son to die on the cross, to save us from our sins.

Sing or recite—

> Jesus, may we ever be
> Those who truly worship Thee;
> Serving Thee while life is given;
> Saved at last with Thee in heaven.

What is the Third Commandment?

Thou shalt not take the name of the Lord thy God in vain; for the Lord will not hold him guiltless that taketh His name in vain.

What is it to take God's name in vain?

To speak it in a profane or careless manner.

Sing or recite—

> May I never speak thy name
> Lightly, or with lips profane.
> May the name of Jesus be
> Life, and peace, and joy to me.

What is the Fourth Commandment?

Remember the Sabbath day to keep it holy. Six days shalt thou labor and do all thy work. But the seventh day is the Sabbath of the Lord thy God: in it thou shalt not do any work, thou, nor thy son, nor thy daughter, thy man-servant, nor thy maid-servant, nor thy cattle, nor thy stranger that is within thy gates. For in six days the Lord made heaven and earth, the sea, and all that in them is, and rested the seventh day. Wherefore the Lord blessed the Sabbath day and hallowed it.

What is it to keep the Sabbath day holy?

Not to play or work, as we do on week days, but attend Church and Sunday School when it is possible to do so, and think much about God.

How many days are there in the week? Yes; seven. So God only asks us to devote *one* day out of seven alone to Him, which is very reasonable, is it not? It is not hard to think all day long of our dear parents, and sisters, and brothers; if we love them, we cannot help doing so. Then, if we love God, it will not be hard to think of Him all day

day Sunday, and week days, too; think of what He has given us, and done for us, and promised us. Let us *remember* His commands.

Sing or recite—

> May the day which Thou has blest,
> Be to me a day of rest—
> Free from labor and from care—
> Spent with God in praise and prayer.

What is the Fifth Commandment?

Honor thy father and thy mother, that thy days may be long upon the land which the Lord thy God giveth thee.

What is it to *honor* your parents?

To love and obey them, and respect their wishes, as well as their commands.

What *promise* is made to those who keep this commandment?

They shall live long upon the land which God gives them.

Sing or recite—

> May our parents ever be
> Loved with all sincerity,
> Honored in their least command,
> And we dwell long upon the land.

What is the Sixth Commandment?

Thou shalt not kill.

Is there more than one way to break this commandment?

There is—to wish any one dead, or to fail to do anything in our power to save life.

Sing or recite—

> Jesus gives us life and breath;
> Jesus, keep us safe from death.
> When He wants us, then, in love,
> He will take us up above.

What is the Seventh Commandment?

Thou shalt not commit adultery.

What does this mean?

Not to think, say, or do any impure thing. Little children should never say or do anything they would not like their parents and Jesus to see and hear.

Sing or recite—

> May our hearts and lives be pure;
> May we to the end endure.
> Jesus promised such should see
> God, through all eternity.

66

What is the Eighth Commandment?

Thou shalt not steal.

What does this mean?

Not to take things that belong to other people.

[Speak of taking *little* things at home—sugar, pennies, etc.—and from orchards, gardens, stores, etc.]

Sing or recite—

> Keep us, Jesus, should we feel
> Sa an tempting us to steal!
> May we learn to trust in Thee,
> And from evil be kept free.

What is the Ninth Commandment?

Thou shalt not bear false witness against thy neighbor.

What does this mean?

To say anything that is not true of any one; to try and injure them.

Sing or recite—

> May our words be always true;
> Lord, our every thought renew!
> And may every action be
> Honest toward man and Thee.

What is the Tenth Commandment?

Thou shalt not covet thy neighbor's house; thou shalt not covet thy neighbor's wife, nor his man-servant, nor his maid-servant, nor his ox, nor his ass, nor anything that is thy neighbor's.

What does this mean?

Not to want or long for anything that belongs to another.

[Tell the story of Ahab, and any other you know of, to illustrate what covetousness leads to.]

Sing or recite—

> All we have from God is sent;
> What we have is only lent—
> Daily breath and daily food—
> Give us, Lord, what seemeth good!

PRIMARY CLASS EXERCISE.

WHAT were all you little folks made for?
To learn to do God's will, and get ready for heaven.

Where do we learn God's will?

In the Holy Bible.

Whom does God *want* to go to heaven?

Every one.

Does God love every one?

Yes; "God so loved the world that He gave His only begotten Son, that *whosoever* believeth in Him should not perish, but have everlasting life."

Sing page 111, CHARM—

"I am so glad that our Father in heaven."

Do all people love God?

They do not?

Then, will God take every one to heaven?

Only those who love and serve Him here.

Why do not all people love God?

Because they have wicked hearts.

Can we go to heaven with wicked hearts?
We can not.
What, then, must we do?
Have our hearts changed.
How can we do this?
Ask God, for Christ's sake, to make our hearts pure and clean.

[Offer this prayer: "Create in me a clean heart, O God, and renew a right spirit within me."]

Sing page 11, PURE GOLD—

"I will pray."

Will not God give us clean hearts without asking?
He will not.
Why?
Because He wants us to feel the need of it first.
When our hearts are once clean, will they not stay so?
Not unless we watch and pray.
Can we keep good, by only watching?
No; we must pray also.
To whom must we pray?
To God.

70

For what must we pray?
The Holy Spirit.
What can the Holy Spirit do?
Help us to be good.

"When He, the Spirit of Truth, is come, He will guide you into all truth."

Sing page 99, SONGS FOR LITTLE ONES—

"I'm a little pilgrim."

Will God send the Holy Spirit, if we ask Him?
Yes; for Jesus promised it.
What is another name for the Holy Spirit?
The Comforter.
What can the Holy Spirit do for us when we are troubled?
Comfort us.
What when we are weak and afraid?
Make us strong.
What when we are foolish?
Make us wise.
Can we always have the Holy Spirit?
We can.
How do you know we can?
Because Jesus said it would abide with us.

"And I will pray the Father, and He shall give you

another Comforter, that He may abide with you forever."—
John xiv. 16.

Sing or recite page 31—

"Jesus has said it."

When we believe the word of Jesus what do
we have?

Faith.

Will He be pleased with us if we do not
believe?

No; for "without faith it is impossible to
please Him."

How may we be sure we love Jesus?

If we keep His commandments.

How old must we be to love Jesus and keep
His commandments?

Old enough to love our parents and obey them.

Does Jesus want such little ones to love Him?

He does.

Did He ever say anything about *little*
children?

Yes; "Suffer the little children to come
unto Me and forbid them not; for of such is
the kingdom of heaven."

Sing page 31, SONGS FOR LITTLE ONES—

"Saviour, like a shepherd lead us."

T HE Lord is my shepherd; I shall not want.

2. He maketh me to lie down in green pastures; He leadeth me beside the still waters.

3. He restoreth my soul; He leadeth me in the paths of righteousness for His name's sake.

4. Yea, though I walk through the valley of the shadow of death, I will fear no evil· for Thou art with me; Thy rod and Thy staff they comfort me.

5. Thou preparest a table for me in the presence of mine enemies; Thou anointest my head with oil; my cup runneth over.

6. Surely goodness and mercy shall follow me all the days of my life; and I will dwell in the house of the Lord forever.

A LITTLE LESSON.

HOW many disciples did Jesus first choose? Twelve.

What were their names?

Simon Peter and his brother Andrew; James and John, whose father's name was Zebedee; Philip and Bartholomew, Thomas and Matthew; James, whose father's name was Alpheus; Thaddeus, Simon, and Judas Iscariot.

What were they called?

The twelve apostles.

What does the word "apostle" mean?

One sent forth.

For what did He send them forth?

To tell the world about Him (Jesus).

What about Him?

That He had come to save them from their sins.

How many apostles were afterward sent forth?

Seventy.

Who was called the *great* apostle?

Paul.

What was his name before he was converted?

Saul.

How did he feel toward Christians before his conversion?

He hated and persecuted them. [Tell how.]

Why did he feel and act so?

Because he had a wicked heart, and did not love Jesus.

How was his heart changed?

Jesus called to him and showed him how wicked he was.

Did he listen to the voice?

He listened and obeyed; then God forgave his sins and made his heart pure and clean.

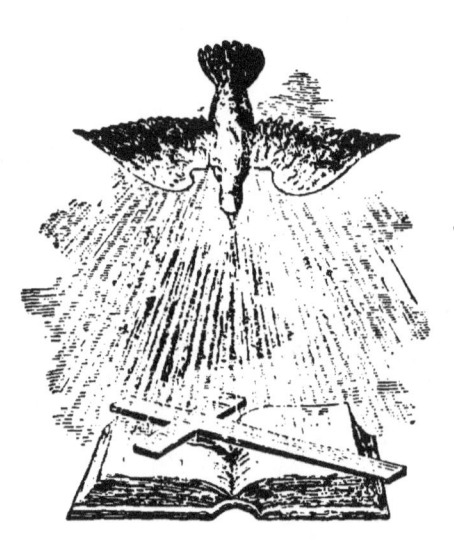

ANNIVERSARY HYMN.

THIS pleasant Anniversary Day
   We hail with cheerful lays,
And gratitude to Him who taught
   Young hearts to sing His praise.

O, may·we through the coming year
   Each golden hour improve;
Storing our little minds with truth,
   And our little hearts with love—

Love for our little schoolmates,
   Love for our teachers dear,
And love for our blessed Saviour,
   Who loves and meets us here.

If we confess our sins, He is faithful and just to for- give us our sins and to cleanse us from all un- righteousness.

1 John i. 9.

78

RECITATION FOR A VERY LITTLE GIRL.

I DON'T think I *care* to say but a word,
For they say "Little folks should be seen
    and not heard."
But you need not to think, *because* we are small,
That we don't know as much as *some* big folks,
    THAT'S ALL.

JOE'S VALENTINE.

I SEE your little smiling eyes,
Brighten up with glad surprise;
It only is St. Valentine,
Called to drop another line;
So here's a kiss, and off I go,
But leave my heart with little Joe.

79

EDDIE'S LITTLE BROTHER.

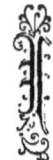 HAVE a darling little brother,
   Just as sweet
And cute as any other
   On our street.

He jumps and laughs and crows;
   Cries, sometimes, too,
'Cause that's the only way he knows
   How to say "don't" or "do."

He has black hair, and eyes to match;
   A little nose;
Ten little fingers that can scratch,—
   Ten little toes.

God sent him to our house one day;
   How glad was I!
I hope He'll let him always stay,
   And never die.

Dear little Walter! (that's his name)
   While we're together,
No one shall ever teaze or blame
   My little brother.

DAYS IN THE MONTH.

ANUARY has *Thirty-one*,
 Snow and ice, and lots of fun.

FEBRUARY has *Twenty-eight*,
In which to slide, and sleigh, and skate;
But every fourth year the records incline
To add to the number, and make *Twenty-nine*.

MARCH has also *Thirty-one*,
In which we have more wind than fun.

APRIL, with its sun and showers,
Has *Thirty* for its leaves and flowers.

MAY, with frolic and with fun,
Fills up the number *Thirty-one*.

Only *Thirty* we have in JUNE;
Its roses and sunshine are gone *so* soon!

Remember now thy Creator in the days of thy youth.

Ec. xii. 1.

DAYS IN THE MONTH.—Continued.

JULY again brings *Thirty-one*,
And we toss the hay 'neath the Summer sun.

AUGUST has *Thirty-one* as well;
Hear the harvest chorus swell!

SEPTEMBER, with *Thirty*, is calm and still,
And does *its* work in the busy mill.

Of days to climb, and jump, and run,
OCTOBER contributes *Thirty-one*.

NOVEMBER is so dreary and cold,
I'm GLAD *it* has only *Thirty* all told.

Hurrah! for Christmas comes in DECEMBER,
And *it* has *Thirty-one*, I remember.

So teach us
to number our
days,
that we may
apply
our hearts unto
wisdom.

Psalm xc. 12.

CHRISTMAS RHYMES.

ERHAPS you think I am too small
 To be of any use at all.
 You're much mistaken, though; for I
 Can do *lots*, if I only try.

But I can *play* best of anything—
I can use a top and string;
Walk on stilts and look *so tall*,
And very seldom have a fall;
Fly a kite, and jump and run,
And every day have lots of fun.

I can study, too, as well;
Read a little bit, and spell;
Write some on my slate, and sing;
But the *best* of everything
Comes on Sunday—then I go
To the Sunday School, you know.
O, I didn't mean to say
Sunday was better than *Christmas day!*
For then our dear old friend Kris Kringle
Comes along with a merry jingle,
And if we've been good all the year,
He'll not forget us, never fear.
I really think he's coming now,
So I must hurry and make my bow.

ANNIVERSARY EXERCISE.

GOD be merciful unto us and bless us; and cause His face to shine upon us.— *Psalm lxvii.* 1.

O GIVE thanks unto the Lord, for He is good; for His mercy endureth forever.—*Psalm cvii.* 1.

DEPART from evil and do good; seek peace and pursue it.—*Psalm xxxiv.* 14.

I WILL arise and go to my father, and will say unto him, Father, I have sinned against heaven and before thee, and am no more worthy to be called thy son.— *Luke xv.* 18.

SEEK ye the Lord while He may be found; call ye upon Him while He is near.— *Isa. lv.* 6.

86

L ITTLE children, keep yourselves from idols.—1 *John v.* 21.

O SING unto the Lord a new song.— *Psalm xcvi.* 1.

V ERILY I say unto you, except ye be converted and become as little children, ye shall not enter into the kingdom of heaven.—*Matt. xviii.* 3.

E VERY good and perfect gift is from above.—*James i.* 17.

Recite or sing—

> God is love, and little children
> Have His tender, watchful care;
> He will not forsake or leave us,
> But go w th us everywhere.

[To be recited by nine small children, as near a size as possible, wearing large cards (suspended from their necks by ribbon or cord) bearing the initial letters, and turned as each verse is given—as in the beautiful exercise, of which one never wearies, " Feed my lambs."]

www.ingramcontent.com/pod-product-compliance
Lightning Source LLC
Chambersburg PA
CBHW020046030726
47499CB00007B/2614